Modern Curriculum Press
BEGINNING
TO
READ
Series

Forgetful Farmer Fred

Craig L. Tweedt
Joy Ann Tweedt
Alvin Granowsky
Illustrated by Michael L. Denman

MODERN CURRICULUM PRESS
Cleveland • Toronto

13900 Prospect Road, Cleveland, Ohio 44136.

Softcover edition published simultaneously in Canada by Globe/ Modern Curriculum Press, Toronto.

Library of Congress Cataloging in Publication Data

Tweedt, Craig L., 1950-
Forgetful Farmer Fred.

Summary: Farmer Fred is so forgetful that he sometimes neglects important chores, until he buys a computer to remind him of what to do.
1. Children's stories, American. (1. Farm life — Fiction. 2. Memory — Fiction. 3. Computers — Fiction) I. Tweedt, Joy Ann, 1951- . II. Granowsky, Alvin, 1936- III. Denman, Michael L., ill. IV. Title.
PZ7.T896Fo 1985 (E) 85-8837

ISBN 0-8136-5166-2
ISBN 0-8136-5666-4 (pbk.)

1 2 3 4 5 6 7 8 9 10 87 86 85

Farmer Fred worked very hard. But he had one big problem. Fred was forgetful.

Farmer Fred had many things to do around the farm. Every day — no matter how hard he tried — Forgetful Farmer Fred forgot something.

Forgetful Farmer Fred forgot something even when his son, Frank, tried to help him remember. "Dad forgot something again," Frank would often say.

Forgetful Farmer Fred forgot something even when his wife, Francis, tried to remind him.

"My husband is just a little forgetful," Francis would explain to her friends.

Sometimes Forgetful Fred forgot to let the horses out in the right field.

At times Forgetful Fred forgot to feed the pigs.

Forgetful Farmer Fred often forgot to collect the chicken eggs.

And there were days when Forgetful Fred forgot to put gas in the tractor.

Time and again he would forget to put the cows in the barn at night.

Whenever Forgetful Farmer Fred forgot something, everyone was upset.

One day Frank came home from school very excited. "Dad! Dad! I found something that will help you never forget anything again!"

"That sounds wonderful," said Forgetful Farmer Fred. "I need help. I can't even remember what I forgot today."

Frank told his father what the teacher had said about computers.

"A computer can remember thousands of things. You type information into the computer. The computer stores the information in its memory until you need it. You can make lists and the computer will remember them for you. You can even change the lists or add to them!"

"If you can make it work, we will try a computer," said Forgetful Farmer Fred as he fell asleep in his favorite chair.

The next morning, Frank and his father went to a computer store.

They saw many kinds of computers. Finally, they found one that would help Forgetful Farmer Fred.

F
ZAPPO

Frank set up the computer.
Then he typed in all the information about the farm.

Forgetful Farmer Fred was sure that all the things on the farm were too much for a machine to remember.

BUT IT DID REMEMBER!

Every day the computer would print a list of all the things Fred had to do that day.

The computer told Farmer Fred when to do his regular chores.

And the computer helped Fred remember his special chores, too.

Frank and Francis were delighted. They didn't have to remind Farmer Fred to feed the pigs or put the cows in the barn.

Farmer Fred let the horses out in the right pasture. And he collected the chicken eggs.

He even remembered to put gas in his tractor.

orgetful Farmer Fred remembered
rything with the help of his computer.
s friends no longer called him Forgetful
rmer Fred. From then on, Fred had a
v name — Faithful Farmer Fred.